THE NUNS

The play is set in Haiti at the time of the first negro
revolt in 1804. Three nuns are hiding away in an abandoned warehouse, where they are waiting for the
arrival of a wealthy noblewoman, whom they have
promised to hide and help escape from the island.
The first shock for the audience is the realisation
that the nuns are all played by men. But in addition,
their behaviour seems more suitable to a thieves
kitchen than to the cloister, and as the action unrolls,
we are treated to a ceremony of surprise and horror,
where the voodoo drums beating in the distance have
a subtle influence on the unrolling of this macabre play.
This is a theatre that is often reminiscent of Artaud
and Genet, poetical, expressionistic and highly dramatic, bringing philosophical and symbolic meaning
into a dramatic situation of great intensity.

Eduardo Manet is a young Cuban writer, now living
in Paris and writing in French, who has achieved
international fame with this play, the most successful
drama of its type during the Paris 1969 season, where
it enjoyed an exceptionally long run. The British
premiere was given at the Sussex Arts Centre with
Patrick Wymark and Dudley Foster in the leading
roles, produced by Walter Eysselinck.

PLAYSCRIPT 43

'the nuns'

eduardo manet
TRANSLATED BY ROBERT BALDICK

CALDER AND BOYARS · LONDON

First published in France 1969
by Editions Gallimard

© Editions Gallimard

This translation first published in Great Britain 1970
by Calder and Boyars Ltd
18 Brewer Street London W1R 4AS

© Robert Baldick 1970

All performing rights in this play
are strictly reserved and applications
for performance should be made to
PL Representation Limited
33 Sloane Street London SW1

No performance of the play may
be given unless a licence has been
obtained prior to rehearsal.

ISBN 0 7145 0721 0 Cloth Edition
ISBN 0 7145 0722 9 Paper Edition

Printed by photo-lithography
and made at the Pitman Press,
Bath.

EDUARDO MANET was born in Havana, Cuba, in 1927, and studied philosophy, literature, drama and cinema at the University of Havana. In 1950 he came to Europe, where he studied drama in Paris with Etienne Decroux, Pierre Valde, Tania Balachova and Jacques Lecoq, and attended courses in Italian literature and Etruscology at Perugia, Florence and Rome. After writing a number of scripts for French television, he returned to Cuba in 1960. There he became Director General of the Cuban National Theatre Company, and a script-writer and director at the Cinema Institute, where he assisted Chris Marker in the filming of 'Cuba, si'. He directed four full-length films and six shorts, one of which, 'El Negro', was chosen in London as one of the ten best films of its year. He also wrote two novels in French, 'Les Etrangers dans la ville' and 'Un Cri sur le Rivage'. He is at present living in Paris and working on a new play, provisionally entitled 'Them'.

ROBERT BALDICK was born in Huddersfield of a French mother and an English father, and educated at Oxford. He is a Fellow of Pembroke College, Oxford, joint editor of the Penguin Classics, and a Fellow of the Royal Society of Literature. His published works include several biographies, a history of duelling, and a study of the siege of Paris; and he has translated the books of a wide range of authors from Flaubert to Simenon, and Chateaubriand to Sartre. Among notable plays he has translated are Montherlant's Queen in Death, Schehade's Vasco, and Barrault's Rabelais. He is married to the American translator Jacqueline Baldick.

THE NUNS

THE NUNS was first performed as LES NONNES on 5 May 1969 at the Theatre de Poche-Montparnasse, Paris, with the following cast:

MOTHER SUPERIOR	Etienne Bierry
SISTER ANGELA	Andre Julien
SISTER INES	Pierre Byland
SENORA	Suzel Goffre

The play was directed by Roger Blin

THE NUNS was first performed in this translation on 12 March 1970 at the Gardner Centre for the Arts, University of Sussex, Brighton, with the following cast:

MOTHER SUPERIOR	Patrick Wymark
SISTER ANGELA	Dudley Foster
SISTER INES	Bernard Hopkins
SENORA	Marian Diamond

The play was directed by Walter Eysselinck

PART ONE

(The play is set in Haiti at the time of the first
Negro revolt.

The scene is a cellar in an abandoned warehouse. There is a little door on the left, leading outside and another on the right. There
are sacks piled up in the corners and ropes
hanging from the ceiling.

Various odd objects (a headless dummy for
example) are littered about the stage. In the
centre there is a niche containing a crudely
carved crucifix, almost a totem. The overall
impression is of a primitive catacomb.

Gregorian chants can be heard which stop when
the curtain goes up.

The MOTHER SUPERIOR is sitting at a little
table loaded with food and drink. Her sleeves
are rolled up and she is eating with her fingers.
She motions to SISTER INES, who is standing
beside her, to pour her some more wine.

SISTER INES carries out her order. SISTER
ANGELA comes in.

The MOTHER SUPERIOR, SISTER INES and
SISTER ANGELA are men. The MOTHER
SUPERIOR is a muscular specimen of the big,
red-faced type who, if he goes on eating and
drinking at the same rate, will have an obese
and unhealthy old age.

SISTER INES is the youngest of the three, little
more than an adolescent, with nervous gestures which reveal an inherent instability.

SISTER ANGELA is thin, wiry, level-headed.

Throughout the play, the nuns' voices and
gestures remain natural and masculine).

SISTER ANGELA. (to the MOTHER SUPERIOR)
You think everything will go all right?

MOTHER SUPERIOR. (with her mouth full) Everything ... fine.

SISTER ANGELA. You don't think there'll be any
hitches?

MOTHER SUPERIOR. No trouble at all.

SISTER ANGELA. (taking a cigar out of her pocket,
rolling it between her palms, biting off the
end, spitting it out, and putting the cigar in
her mouth) You may think so, but I don't like
it when things look too easy.

MOTHER SUPERIOR. A philosopher would say you
were a pessimist by nature.

SISTER ANGELA. Oh, you think everything's as
easy as pie ... Well, we've found out often
enough that it isn't.

MOTHER SUPERIOR. Sister Angela, I put my trust
in the Lord.

SISTER ANGELA. Oh, so it's the Lord, is it, who's
going to get me burnt at the stake if I don't
watch out? The more I think about it, the more
I reckon it isn't the Lord that's lousing things
up, it's you.

MOTHER SUPERIOR. (licking her fingers) The ways
of the Lord are hard to understand. I am but a
humble tool in his divine hands.

(She motions to SISTER INES to clear away,
and takes a last drink of wine.
SISTER INES goes out, staggering under the
weight of the little table and its contents).

SISTER ANGELA. That's right - let's all pretend
the Lord's guiding you and you can hear him,
when it's more likely that he's talking and you're
not even listening.

MOTHER SUPERIOR. Sister Angela, are our nerves
just a little bit ragged today?

SISTER ANGELA. Oh, go to hell!

MOTHER SUPERIOR. (wagging her finger at her)
Tut-tut-tut! No bad language here, if you don't
mind. If you want to be useful, why don't you
give me one of those cigars you seem to enjoy
so much? It'll help to settle my supper.

SISTER ANGELA. (grumpily taking out a cigar and
handing it to her) Yes, you're right, my nerves
are all shot to pieces. What's the use of deny-
ing it? After all, how many weeks has it taken
to get everything ready?

MOTHER SUPERIOR. (who has taken the cigar,
sniffed it, and cut the end off with a pair of
scissors, puts it in her mouth and motions to
SISTER ANGELA to light it for her) Exactly
ninety-three days. You'd do better to think

about the poor devils who are thrown into
prison or sent to the galleys for years and
years, or even a lifetime ...

SISTER ANGELA. (lighting the MOTHER SUPERIOR's
cigar) Oh, I know it doesn't seem a long time to
you. But then, you can doll yourself up like a
lady and get out of here. You can breathe the
fresh air outside. You go to dinner-parties,
you sleep in soft beds, and I wouldn't mind
betting you have a bit of the old ...

MOTHER SUPERIOR. Watch it, Sister Angela! That
sort of language will be the ruin of you. Once
you let your tongue run away with you like
that, you may find that you can't control it
when you have to. I might add that if I've gone
out, it was for the common good; if I've breathed
the fresh air outside, it was because somebody has to see to this business; and if I've been
to dinner-parties, that was because our plans
required me to ... (draws on her cigar and
blows out the smoke) As for your last suppos-
ition, I refuse even to consider it. It's unworthy
of the mutual trust which has to exist between
us. And finally ... (she stands up and towers
over SISTER ANGELA) ... if you were so un-
happy about things, why didn't you do something about it? Why didn't you volunteer to help?

SISTER ANGELA. Oh, I'm no good at all at that
society stuff - you've said so yourself. It
makes me sick, bowing and scraping and licking
people's boots.

MOTHER SUPERIOR. Then it's all agreed. Each of

us does the job she's cut out for: I plan the
operation, you carry it out, and Sister Ines
looks after the incidentals ... (looking nos-
talgically at the door through which SISTER
INES has gone out) Poor Sister Ines! I sometimes wonder why the Lord picks his most
innocent creatures to try them with suffering.
I sometimes wonder whether her deaf-and-
dumb condition is a punishment or a blessing.

SISTER ANGELA. (literally flinging herself into a
small armchair, and lying back with her legs
apart and a cigar in her mouth) You might
help to solve the problem by giving her a bit
less work and not treating her so badly.

MOTHER SUPERIOR. Sister Angela, you aren't
in tune with the spirit of our time. You're in-
capable of grasping the philosophical ideas
which govern the progress of mankind. There
are contradictions in Nature which sometimes
create the most peculiar contrasts. What seems
to be a bad thing turns out to be good ... and
what seems to be a good thing may very well be
bad. For instance, take the lives of the deaf-
mutes of this world, the blind, the crippled,
the diseased, the arthritics, the syphilitics.
People hate them because they are the living
image of sickness and misery, because they
are a reminder that ugliness, unhappiness and
poverty can swoop down on anybody at any time.
People despise them because they are weak,
because they aren't equipped to fight for their
lives in this vile, wicked world. That's why
the existence of all those poor creatures is an
endless martyrdom. Now you know how much

I appreciate the delicate nature, the spiritual purity, the exquisite timidity of little Sister Ines - but what would happen if we showed her nothing but understanding, kindness and affection? What would happen if - God forbid! the day should come when she had to face the grim struggle for survival alone and unprotected? She'd be done for - that's what. Deprived of the love and comfort she had known before, she would find herself defenceless, helpless, exposed to the most appalling dangers. That is why now and then - but not often, far less often than you suggest - I treat her rather harshly, and why I take the trouble to teach her dozens of little jobs which may be very useful to her in the future. In other words, the good I'm doing her may seem bad, but it isn't half as bad as the bad times - the really bad times - she's going to have one day. And what does she think about it herself? Just look at her!

(SISTER INES has just come in, smiling sweetly.)

Fresh as a daisy, sweet as honey, ready to serve me - or you, for that matter - with a willing heart.

(The MOTHER SUPERIOR turns round and sits down. SISTER INES places a cushion at her feet and sits down on it. The MOTHER SUPERIOR strokes her face. SISTER INES picks up a guitar and starts playing it softly).

If fate had smiled on her, Sister Ines would have blossomed in some noble household, in the midst of a select, refined society ...

SISTER ANGELA. (who had been listening with only
half an ear to the MOTHER SUPERIOR's
speech) You really think she'll follow your
directions?

MOTHER SUPERIOR. (with feigned surprise) Who?
The Senora? Of course she will - otherwise all
my work would be wasted, all those dinner-
parties that upset you so much, all the hours
and hours I've spent listening to her talk ...
Because I must say, Sister Angela, that when
it comes to talking, she beats me hands down!
What a woman! It's practically impossible to
shut her up. For a while I was afraid I was
never going to be able to get a word in edge-
ways in all her gabble ... But as I've already
told you, Sister Angela, God gave human beings
intelligence for them to use it. And thanks to
my intelligence I found a way of shutting the
Senora's mouth and opening her ears ... Shall
I tell you what it was? I ... (pause, then her
tone changes) terrified her.

(SISTER INES stops playing, frightened by the
MOTHER SUPERIOR's sinister grimace).

There, there, Sister Ines, my little pet, don't
be frightened, I wasn't talking about you ...
(to SISTER ANGELA) Simple souls are always
frightened by the same old stories. For them
there'll always be dragons and witches and
wolves gobbling up little girls in the woods.
(to SISTER INES) Go on playing your guitar,
dear, while Sister Angela and I are talking.

18

SISTER ANGELA. (yawns noisily, stretches and
stands up) Well, all I can say is, if she swall-
owed a story like that she must be a ruddy idiot.
I always thought society women were stupid,
but I never knew they were that stupid.

(She goes over to a chest, takes out a bottle,
uncorks it and starts drinking).

MOTHER SUPERIOR. Careful, Sister Angela,
alcohol leaves an undesirable smell in the air .
I grant you that the Senora, like all great ladies,
is a bit soft in the head and not very bright, but
all the same we shouldn't ask too much of human
innocence. So we've got to keep up the austere
appearance of our holy condition. Besides, it's
nearly time for her to get here. (She gets up)
Sister Ines ... (She explains herself in gestures
at the same time as she speaks)... tidy the place
up ... Clear all this away ... Take this! (Gives
her the cigar) I don't want any smoke hanging
around. Are you going to put that bottle away
sometime, Sister Angela? And when you've
finished here, Sister Ines, go and get the
incense. There's nothing like it for sanctifying
the premises and getting rid of bad smells at
the same time.

(SISTER INES starts cleaning up the cellar).

SISTER ANGELA. (takes last swig of the wine and
puts the bottle away) I needed that to get ready
for your clouds of incense. The smell of the
stuff makes me sick.

MOTHER SUPERIOR. I must admit it has a pene-

trating odour. Our ancestors knew what they
were doing when they used it in large quanti-
ties to neutralise the noxious exhalations of
soul and body. The fact that we put up with it
without enjoying it only makes our behaviour
doubly meritorious. Now if we liked the smell
of incense, we might be suspected of connivance
with ... (she draws closer to SISTER ANGELA
and lowers her voice) ... the Devil. (She
crosses herself).

ISTER ANGELA. (looking her straight in the eyes)
Are you thinking of trying your terror tech-
nique on me, Reverend Mother?

OTHER SUPERIOR. (with a good-natured laugh)
I'd be wasting my time, Sister Angela ...
(giving her a tremendous slap on the back)
Compared with you I'm just a babe in arms,
yes, just a babe in arms. On the other hand,
with the Senora ... You ought to have seen her
when I told her what was going to happen on the
island - the way her hands started shaking,
her face turned white, her eyes opened wide in
terror!

STER ANGELA. Oh, I wish she'd hurry up with the
stuff so we could get moving! I'd like to see her
here and doing what you tell her.

OTHER SUPERIOR. Sister Angela, how can you be
so lacking in artistic feeling? One has to do
these things slowly, gently, with patience and
finesse. What sort of a world would it be if

SISTER ANGELA. I don't know what sort of a world
it'd be, but I do know what'll happen if our
plans come unstuck. You haven't forgotten,
Reverend Mother, what's in store for us if the'
find us out and catch us?

MOTHER SUPERIOR. (trying to banish such painful
ideas, starts moving about) Come now, Sister
Angela, I haven't forgotten the circumstances
we happen to be in ...

SISTER ANGELA. You'd better not forget either,
because if you go on behaving as if this was
just a picnic you're going to wake up in a dungeon with the rats eating your backside away .

MOTHER SUPERIOR. Sister Angela, I wish you
wouldn't use such crude language.

SISTER ANGELA. (following her) And they don't
chuck you in a dungeon before making you own
up first to everything you've done or haven't
done ...

MOTHER SUPERIOR. (moving things about and
chanting to herself) Kyrie eleison, kyrie
eleison ...

SISTER ANGELA. ... and for getting confessions,
there's nothing better than the rack ... You
know what I'm talking about, don't you, Rever'
Mother? The ropes biting into your flesh ...

MOTHER SUPERIOR. Sister Angela!

21

SISTER ANGELA. (following her up and down the
    stage in all directions) Your arms and legs
    beginning to crack ...

MOTHER SUPERIOR. Stop it, Sister ...

SISTER ANGELA. Your skin tearing ... your bones
    breaking ...

MOTHER SUPERIOR. There's no need to ...

SISTER ANGELA. And even then you can count your-
    self lucky to be on the rack. Because there's
    other things ...

MOTHER SUPERIOR. You're going too far, Sister
    Angela!

SISTER ANGELA. There's the garrotte, a shameful,
    agonising death ... There's the axe ...

MOTHER SUPERIOR. I order you to ...

SISTER ANGELA. ... that chops off your head with
    a single blow. And then they put your head on
    show as a sort of dreadful warning ...

MOTHER SUPERIOR. (trying to push past SISTER
    ANGELA) I've been very patient so far ...

SISTER ANGELA. But in our case, you know the way
    they'll choose to finish us off, don't you!

MOTHER SUPERIOR. (stopping her ears and
    shouting) I can't hear a thing! You can say

what you like - I can't hear a thing!

SISTER ANGELA. (shouting louder than the MOTHER
SUPERIOR) The stake, Reverend Mother, the
stake! Your skin roasting and the fat melting
inside you ...

MOTHER SUPERIOR. I can't hear!

SISTER ANGELA. The heat gradually drying up your
blood ...

MOTHER SUPERIOR. (crossing herself and making
the sign of the Cross towards SISTER ANGELA)
Vade retro! Go away! Vade retro!

SISTER ANGELA. (flinging herself on the MOTHER
SUPERIOR and pinning her arms down in a
wrestling hold) ... and your body turning to
ashes before your very eyes ...

MOTHER SUPERIOR. (slowly falling to her knees)
Have pity on me! Have pity on me!

SISTER ANGELA. (bending over her and still
gripping her arms) ... a little pile of ashes
they'll just scatter in the wind ...

MOTHER SUPERIOR. (getting to her feet with a
tremendous effort) That's enough! You harpy!
You monster! Do you want to bring bad luck on
us? You'd like everything to go wrong, wouldn
you, you're so full of bile! I ought to punch a
hole in your liver to let out the poison. Go on,
spew out your venom, spew it out!

(The MOTHER SUPERIOR is now on top of
SISTER ANGELA and trying to throttle her.
At this moment SISTER INES comes in and
runs happily around the stage swinging her
censer and filling the air with incense.
The MOTHER SUPERIOR and SISTER ANGELA
break apart and start coughing).

MOTHER SUPERIOR. What the devil's that? (she
    coughs) Is the little fool trying to smoke us
    out ?

SISTER ANGELA. You asked for a (coughs) cloud
    of incense, didn't you? (Coughs) Well, you've
    got it.

    (SISTER INES comes back across the stage,
    still swinging the censer).

MOTHER SUPERIOR. And she's giving us some
    more! (Coughs) Get out! Go on, scarper! Get
    out of here! Out!

    (She runs out, pushing SISTER INES in front
    of her. SISTER ANGELA starts fanning the air
    with an old sack.
    The MOTHER SUPERIOR comes in with a huge
    scent-spray and starts spraying the stage).

MOTHER SUPERIOR. They say the simple-minded
    go to heaven, but judging by Sister Ines, if
    there's any justice in the after-life, they all
    ought to be sent straight to hell.

SISTER ANGELA. (still fanning the air with her
    sack) Now that's a good idea. We smelt like a

funeral chamber before, and now we smell
like a brothel. (Stops as if an idea has suddenly struck her) Are you trying to make the
Senora feel at home? (The MOTHER SUPERIOR
shrugs her shoulders. SISTER ANGELA tosses
the sack into a corner and says sarcastically)
By the way, did you see what happened to you?

MOTHER SUPERIOR. (pretending not to understand)
What do you mean?

SISTER ANGELA. You got goose-pimples when I
was talking to you.

MOTHER SUPERIOR. I've got a very impression-
able nature. You took advantage of it, that's
all.

SISTER ANGELA. All I want is for you to get one thing
clear: we can't afford to fall down on this job.

MOTHER SUPERIOR. We shan't - you can take my
word for that.

SISTER ANGELA. But if we're going to bring it off,
we've got to go through with it to the very end.
You understand?

MOTHER SUPERIOR. To the very end.

SISTER ANGELA. If we weaken when the time
comes to ...

MOTHER SUPERIOR. We shan't weaken.

(Somebody knocks on a door in the distance,
producing echoes in the cellar).

That's her! Quick! Sister Ines! Come here!
Sister Angela!

SISTER ANGELA. Steady now!

MOTHER SUPERIOR. (in an agitated voice) Steady
my foot. Go and fetch that cretin, will you.
I'll have to open the door myself. Make sure
everything is in order, Sister Angela. (They
start going out through opposite doors. The
MOTHER SUPERIOR turns round) And whatever you do, watch your tongue!

(They go out. The knocking gets louder).

MOTHER SUPERIOR'S VOICE. Coming! Coming!
Here I am.

(SISTER INES comes in, with SISTER ANGELA
pushing her. During her speech SISTER
ANGELA goes on slapping and pushing SISTER
INES who accepts this treatment meekly while
trying to express herself in gestures).

SISTER ANGELA. Get a move on, you great booby!
So you're not satisfied with poisoning us with
your filthy incense - you've got to start cook-
ing a bloody meal! Now look at you - a ruddy
shambles, that's what you are. Pull your
sleeves down ... Fix your hood ... You're
going to be introduced to a lady, a real live
lady. Do you understand, you ninny? For the
first time in your life you're going to meet a

lady. And for God's sake take that stupid look off your face, or you'll louse the whole thing up.

MOTHER SUPERIOR'S VOICE. Mind the steps.

SENORA'S VOICE. Heavens above, how dark it is down here! Give me your hand, Reverend Mother.

SISTER ANGELA. (to SISTER INES, pinching her) Quick ... Head up, shoulders back ... Now smile, damn you, so the Senora isn't frightened.

(SISTER ANGELA motions to SISTER INES to imitate her. She tries to smile sweetly, but only produces a sinister grimace).

MOTHER SUPERIOR. (coming in) It wasn't as easy as you thought, was it? But here we are ...

SENORA. (off-stage) How on earth do you manage to live down here (coming in) Reverend Mother?

(She is a woman of striking beauty, wearing a long cape with a hood. She is carrying a small chest in one hand).

MOTHER SUPERIOR. With faith, discipline and good will, one can put up with anything, my child.

(The SENORA walks to the centre of the stage. She throws back her hood, and her beauty is fully revealed to the audience).

SENORA. This damp air ... these sad surroundings ... this peculiar smell ...

(She notices the other two nuns).

MOTHER SUPERIOR. Sister Angela ... Sister Ines ... Two little sisters of mercy, without whom the rigours of daily life would have been quite unbearable.

SENORA. Oh, without human sympathy, Mother, the world would be an impossible place. But you deserve more than sympathy for all the kindness you spread around you.

MOTHER SUPERIOR. You flatter me, my child, you flatter me ... Now make yourself at home. Let me relieve you of this. (Gently takes the case the SENORA is carrying) Would you care for something to eat? We shall have to wait a little while, and it wouldn't be wise for you to get tired before we even set off. Sister Ines, Sister Angela, look after our Senora.

(SISTER INES and SISTER ANGELA come nearer, both of them fascinated by the SENORA, though in different ways).

SISTER ANGELA. Allow me, madam.

(SISTER ANGELA helps her to take off her cape. Her eyes are drawn to the white shoulders and ivory neck which are now revealed. SISTER INES has meanwhile brought over the best armchair, and the SENORA sits down with graceful movements).

SENORA. Thank you, thank you, Sister ... Please
don't worry about me.

MOTHER SUPERIOR. (still holding the small chest)
Worry about you? But they've done nothing
else for days. Especially Sister Angela, who's
worried about exposing your delicate person
to the dangers of the voyage we have to make ...

SENORA. Sister Angela! Her name matches her
intentions. (Using Italian pronunciation) Un
Angelo, that's what she is; but surely we are
all in the same situation? And isn't it infinitely
better for us to expose ourselves to the dangers
of the sea than to the risks of ... of the alter-
native?

MOTHER SUPERIOR. Exactly! That's what I've
been telling them day after day. When the
forces of evil are let loose, God only knows
how far they'll go. New laws destroy the pat-
ient work of centuries. The innocent are pers-
ecuted. Property is seized. Look what's
happening on the mainland: murder, looting,
rape! Men go mad, the streets run with blood,
pity becomes a forgotten word. And before you
know where you are, there's something crawling on top of you, feeling and fumbling ...

SENORA. Oh, Reverend Mother ... don't remind me
of all that ... (she slips into a graceful faint).

MOTHER SUPERIOR. Sister Angela! Sister Ines!
Get some food ... something solid, that's the
best thing in a case like this.

(SISTER INES teeters around, not knowing
what to do and not understanding what is
happening).

SISTER ANGELA. (pushing her) Come along, stupid
... Food ... Drink ... Get something for the
Senora!

(SISTER INES goes out).

SENORA. (in a tiny voice) My smelling salts ... in
the travelling bag.

MOTHER SUPERIOR. (to SISTER ANGELA) Outside in
in the passage ... Quick!

(SISTER ANGELA crosses the stage and goes
out).

MOTHER SUPERIOR. (stands close to the SENORA
and bends forward to stroke her face) Now, my
child, there's nothing to worry about ... Your
Mother Superior's here to make sure nothing
happens to you, so you're quite safe.

SENORA. (rests her head against the MOTHER
SUPERIOR, and taking her hand kisses it)
Oh, Reverend Mother, when I think what might
have happened to me if it hadn't been for your
advice. You know as well as I do - or even
better - that a woman on her own is easy prey
- especially when there's danger around!

(SISTER ANGELA comes in and shows obvious
signs of displeasure at what she sees. She

comes forward and throws the bag at the
SENORA's feet).

SISTER ANGELA. Here's the bag.

(She folds her arms and glares at the other
two. The SENORA looks rather surprised at
her behaviour. The MOTHER SUPERIOR gives
a loud laugh, bends down to pick up the bag
and places it in the SENORA's lap).

MOTHER SUPERIOR. I'm not the only one you have
to thank, my child, Sister Angela, for instance,
has seen to all the practical details. It was she
who won over the good sailor whose boat we are
using for the crossing. And it was she who got
together all the food and clothing we need.

SENORA. Then I ought to be doubly grateful to dear
Sister Angela. Because it can't be very easy for
a nun to see to all those horrible practical
details.

SISTER ANGELA. (still rather sulky, but melting
under the SENORA's charm) It wasn't all that
difficult either. I know a bit about the sea, you
know.

MOTHER SUPERIOR. (hurriedly) Sister Angela comes
from a poor but honest family of fishermen.

SENORA. Well, all I can say is that I don't know
anything about the sea, except that it's full of
waves and fish and that it makes you ill. (She
laughs) Whenever I've been on a sea voyage it's
always been on huge big ships with lots of sails

and oars.

SISTER ANGELA.   Little boats are much safer than big ones. Ours is a sturdy little boat. You won't find her too bad.

SENORA. What is she called, Sister Angela?

SISTER ANGELA. The Reaper.

SENORA. Oh, what an awful name!

SISTER ANGELA. It was her skipper that chose it. The last skipper, I mean. The one that was a smuggler.

MOTHER SUPERIOR.   (sensing the opportunity to cut this conversation short) Here's our little Sister Ines with something to keep the wolf from the door.

(SISTER INES comes in carrying the little table loaded with food and drink).

SENORA. What a feast! Why, there's enough here to feed a regiment!

MOTHER SUPERIOR. Sister Ines must have lost her head when she saw you fainting.

SENORA. But I shan't be able to do justice to all this. I live on next to nothing. (She tastes one of the courses) Oh, how delicious! Sister Ines, you really must give me the recipe!

32

(SISTER INES smiles at her with her usual
stupid expression).

MOTHER SUPERIOR. You mustn't expect her to
answer when you speak to her. Our poor little
sister lost her voice in an unfortunate accident.

SENORA. (raising her hands in horror) Oh, the
poor little thing! How could such an awful thing
happen to such a dear sweet soul?

SISTER ANGELA. (with a laugh) They cut it off with
a knife, right down at the root.

MOTHER SUPERIOR. Sister Angela, spare us the
details, or the Senora's going to go into another
faint.

SENORA. (still eating) Cut it off? How could that
happen?

MOTHER SUPERIOR. (stopping SISTER ANGELA
before she can reply) Oh, it's a sad story! But
quite a common one in the dreadful times we
live in! (Lowering her voice) An evil star is
guiding man's destiny just now ... Passions
run high ... Queer things happen ... Old
scores are settled. (Makes a vague gesture
with her hairy hand) Sister Ines's family were
very distinguished ... They belonged to ...
the aristocracy. (The last words are barely
audible).

SENORA. The poor angel ... And to think that,
seeing her, you would think she knows nothing
of the wickedness of the world. (She takes a

33

goblet the MOTHER SUPERIOR offers her and
drinks out of it).

MOTHER SUPERIOR. When the soul is pure ...

SISTER ANGELA. Besides, they bashed her about so
much she's a half-wit.

SENORA. (laughing) Oh, Sister Angela, I can see
you've got a sharp edge to your tongue ... Look,
here's something to sweeten you. (She hands
her a little cake) But you aren't going to leave
me to eat by myself, are you? Come along,
sisters, help yourselves! ... Reverend Mother,
try some of this delicious food ... Sister
Angela, another cake ... Sister Ines, a little
wine to bring the colour back to your cheeks.

(The MOTHER SUPERIOR and SISTER ANGELA
don't wait to be asked twice, and start eating
and drinking with the SENORA).

SENORA. My husband always says ... always used
to say that a little friendship and joy helps you
to look on the bright side of things. You've no
idea how awful I felt when I came in here ... A
shiver ran down my spine, and I thought to
myself: this cellar looks just like a tomb. Yet
look at us now: four old friends eating and
drinking without an evil thought between us.

MOTHER SUPERIOR. Yes, it's nice and cheerful
here, isn't it? And we can make it even nicer
... Sister Ines, give us a little music, to get
rid of the Senora's gloomy thoughts. (Understanding the MOTHER SUPERIOR's gestures,

SISTER INES picks up her guitar) What you
are going to hear now is something quite out
of the ordinary, because Sister Ines is stone
deaf and doesn't know what music is. (Seeing
the SENORA's astonished expression) Yes,
she's deaf too ... It seems that a shot fired
next to her shattered her eardrums ... But
then, who can tell what is or isn't in this world
of ours? Everything is changing all the time
and merging in a wonderful mixture in which
we can't help seeing the hand of the Lord. Take
music, for instance - why shouldn't our little
Sister Ines possess the secret of the Seraphims?
Maybe what she plays is real harmony and what
we enjoy as music today will be dismissed
tomorrow as noise, nothing but noise.

(Pause while all three listen to the music).

SENORA. You are right: that's how the angels must
play in heaven. Take this, Sister, and drink
your own health.

(The SENORA puts a goblet to SISTER INES's
lips and the nun takes a drink).

SISTER ANGELA. (with a coarse laugh) Watch it!
When the drink gets hold of her she's quite
capable of stripping off and ...

SENORA. Shush! (She motions to the others to be
quiet).

(SISTER ANGELA and the MOTHER SUPERIOR
are taken aback at first. Then the MOTHER

SUPERIOR decides that the SENORA must have been shocked by what SISTER ANGELA has just said, and gets ready to scold her. But before she can say anything, the SENORA speaks).

SENORA. Listen!

(About the time the MOTHER SUPERIOR asked SISTER INES to play the guitar, the sound of drums had begun very softly, gradually growing louder until the audience can now just hear it).

SISTER ANGELA. Those are drums beating ...

MOTHER SUPERIOR. Hush! (She slaps SISTER INES to make her stop playing. There is a pause which is finally broken by a laugh from the MOTHER SUPERIOR) So they are, Sister Angela. It must be one of those pagan feasts of theirs ... What day is it today? Go on, Ines my child, go on playing ... Let's have some heavenly music to counteract that heretical noise.

SISTER ANGELA. (tense and anxious from now on) And let's get on with the eating and drinking! There's nothing better for facing a sea voyage than a full stomach. Eat up and you won't throw up.

(SISTER ANGELA pours out more wine. The SENORA drinks absentmindedly).

SENORA. What time do we leave, Mother Superior?

MOTHER SUPERIOR. At dawn, at cockcrow.

SENORA. I wish I were already on the boat.

SISTER ANGELA. And once you're on board you'll
say: I wish I was already on shore. That's
life: Nobody's ever satisfied with what he's got
or where he is. There's always something
missing ... We've always got to change ...
Come on, drink up!

MOTHER SUPERIOR. (bending over the SENORA and
trying to hide the fact that she too is a little
worried with a nervous laugh) Now, now, my
child, don't start worrying now that you're on
the point of setting off ...

SENORA. (getting up and walking unconsciously
towards the crucifix) I've had some strange
dreams, Reverend Mother, dreams in which I
saw the scenes you described to me so vividly.
They were terrible dreams, and so overpoweri
that I thought I was really experiencing the
things that were happening in front of me ... C
it was horrible, Mother! Feeling, seeing, almc
touching ... And those screams coming from
all sides! Those faces suddenly bursting out of
the darkness in the light of the torches! ...
And I was in the middle of it all ... I wanted to
run away, but I couldn't move ... I wanted to
talk, but I couldn't open my mouth ... I kept
telling myself: You're just dreaming ... It
isn't true ... In a few minutes you'll wake up
in your room ... in your bed ... and Adelaide
will bring in your morning chocolate ... dear

Adelaide ... You'll tell her all about it, and
she'll laugh and say: That's the pork chop
you had for dinner last night! ... But it went
on and on and I didn't wake up ... On the con-
trary, I sank deeper and deeper into the horror
all around me ... I was surrounded by terri-
fying creatures and something was on top of me,
gripping me, stifling me ... stifling ... (she
covers her face with her hands).

(The drums have grown a little louder).

MOTHER SUPERIOR. (with another nervous laugh) Now,
my child, you mustn't let your imagination run
away with you. Maybe ... yes ...' maybe I
exaggerated a little.

SISTER ANGELA. Anyway there's nothing to worry
about any more. As soon as the cock crows,
we scarper. The boat'll be waiting ... and if
we give the skipper what he's asking for the
job ... (Glancing meaningfully at the MOTHER
SUPERIOR).

MOTHER SUPERIOR. (with a quick warning gesture
to SISTER ANGELA) Oh, I'm sure we've nothing
to fear on that score: the Senora will have
thought of ...

SENORA. (leaning against the wall near the crucifix) Yes ... it's all there ... in the little chest.

(The MOTHER SUPERIOR and SISTER ANGELA
exchange glances. Neither is able to avoid
making a greedy gesture with her hands).

MOTHER SUPERIOR. (with a nervous cackle) Cou
... Could we have a look at it? It isn't often
that a humble nun has a chance to set eyes on
such wordly treasures ... Besides, we've got
to divide them up: so much for the skipper of
the boat ... so much for our needs when we
reach a place of refuge ...

SENORA. (with a wave of her hand) Open it up,
Mother, open it up.

(She holds out a key which SISTER ANGELA
seizes eagerly but which is promptly snatched
from her by the MOTHER SUPERIOR. The two
of them clear away everything on the little
table and put the small chest on it facing the
audience.
The MOTHER SUPERIOR opens it. She and
SISTER ANGELA stand there dazzled by the
sight of the jewels. SISTER INES, who has
been watching them, stops playing. The sound
of drums grows a little louder).

MOTHER SUPERIOR. Marvellous!

SISTER ANGELA. God, how they sparkle!

MOTHER SUPERIOR. They're like stars ... like
suns!

SISTER ANGELA. A fortune!

(They speak in little more than a murmur and
without daring to touch the jewels. The SENORA
slowly approaches them).

SENORA. Every one of those jewels is full of memories for me ... They stick to my skin, heavy with pictures of the past ... Some of them are family heirlooms ... others presents from my husband ... others pieces I bought myself ... out of vanity ... boredom ... the pleasure of spending money ... (For a moment she studies the almost mystical ecstasy of the the three nuns) Wait a minute! ... (She comes up to the chest and rummages in it while the others draw back slightly) Let me see ... Yes ... here they are ... Take this, Reverend Mother, as a present ... (She offers her a jewel) This cameo belonged to my husband's mother.

MOTHER SUPERIOR. Oh, Senora, no ... I couldn't possibly ...

SENORA. I insist ... And you, Sister Angela, take this ring ... It belonged to an aunt of mine I was very fond of ...

SISTER ANGELA. (seizing the ring and trying it on each of her fingers to see which one it fits best) How can I thank you?

SENORA. Keep it in memory of her ... As for you, little sister, (to SISTER INES) I should like you to wear this cross always around your neck. (She puts a cross in her hand) A cousin of mine wore it for her first communion and the day she died ... She was a sweet, kind girl. Nobody deserves it more than you ... (She kisses SISTER INES on the cheek and the nun starts crying, hiding her face) What is it? Mother, what's the matter with her?

MOTHER SUPERIOR. Take no notice. It's just
emotion ... and being given a present ... She
isn't used to it ... The simple-minded can't
understand when happiness knocks at their
door: that's why they cry.

SENORA. I thought I'd offended her with my present.

SISTER ANGELA. Offended her! Why, there's folk
who'd give their right arm just to own one of ˇ
these jewels for an hour ...

(A short silence. SISTER ANGELA's vehemence
causes a slight awkwardness).

SENORA. (to MOTHER SUPERIOR) Didn't you say
you wanted to divide the jewels into those for
the journey and those for our living expenses?

MOTHER SUPERIOR. So I did ... Now let's see ...
(Like a child faced with a plateful of cakes, and
not knowing where to begin) This necklace ...
and these earrings ... may be enough for the
skipper of the boat ... And if he haggles a bit,
we could possibly ...

SENORA. (who has been looking tense for a few
moments) Don't you think that awful noise has
grown louder?

(The sound of the drums is in fact a little
louder and the rhythm has speeded up slightly).

MOTHER SUPERIOR. You ought to use your influence with the Government, Senora, to get
them to forbid these noisy demonstrations that
get on people's nerves. It's a well known fact
noise brings out the worst in human beings.
The Government shouldn't allow anything but
religious music ... and one or two foreign
songs perhaps, on high days and holidays ...

SISTER ANGELA. The best thing we can do just now
is get ready for the voyage ... Senora, wouldn't
you like to come and see what we're taking with
us?

MOTHER SUPERIOR. (on a shrill note of anguish)
Not yet! (The others are all startled, especially SISTER ANGELA who shoots a vicious
glance at her) We've got to put aside what we
need for our immediate expenses, and it's
only right and proper that the Senora should be
present ...

SISTER ANGELA. (savagely) It's more right and
proper she checks the stuff we're taking with
us ... Maybe she'll need something we haven't
got ... Maybe she'll decide there's something
we can leave behind ... (going right up to the
MOTHER SUPERIOR) It was all agreed.

SENORA. I'd rather not go. I have complete con-
fidence in you, Sister Angela, when it comes
to practical problems. And in you, Reverend
Mother, when it comes to dividing up the
jewels. (She goes towards the armchair).

MOTHER SUPERIOR. (noticing SISTER ANGELA's aggressive attitude, tries to bring a lighter tone back to the conversation) Perhaps you'd better go and look, Senora. You've no idea how stubborn Sister Angela can be. Besides, you really must keep an eye on your property. We wouldn't want to make a mistake we'd regret later, on the high seas. I'll see to all the rest.

SENORA. (after a moment's hesitation) Very well. Where are the bags?

SISTER ANGELA. (pointing to a door on the right) Over there ... in the next cellar.

(The SENORA glances around her).

SENORA. Reverend Mother, I feel the same sense of foreboding I had when I arrived. How did you manage to stand all this without going mad?

MOTHER SUPERIOR. (her hands full of jewels, almost tragic in her sincerity) Because I kept thinking all the time about a bright future, my child ... a future of idleness and peace.

SENORA. (who has not been listening to her) I should like to be on the boat, Mother.

SISTER ANGELA. (taking her by the hand) Come along. It's getting late. It'll soon be dawn.

(They go out. The sound of the drums grows louder and the rhythm quickens. SISTER INES ,

who has been sitting in a corner weeping and
examining her cross, watches them go by in
astonishment and follows them).

MOTHER SUPERIOR. (gloating over the jewels and
picking them up in handfuls) A fortune! A
thousand years of riches, of blissful nights and
carefree days! To think of all you could buy
with these bracelets! Carriages, maidservants,
footmen! And these two necklaces? They're
worth a couple of sugar plantations at the very
least. With this you could buy the conscience
of a dozen men and the virtue of a score of
women! With that you could obtain a governor-
ship! With this a bishopric! There's enough
here to become a landowner, a general, a
marquis, perhaps even a duchess! There's
enough to live in a great capital where food and
clothes and cards all cost the earth. Where
you can have whatever you like, provided you
pay for it, whether it's lawful or illicit, normal
or perverse, God's work or the Devil's. With
this you can buy what everyone fights for and
few obtain: authority, mastery, power! In a
silly woman's hands these jewels are just
sparkling pebbles and nothing more! In mine
they will grow and multiply! An Empire lies
within my grasp!

(While speaking she has been putting on the
jewels, on her hands and arms, on her head,
on her clothing. The low sinister sound of the
drums has grown gradually louder. The rhythm
has nothing festive about it. Hypnotised by the
jewels, the MOTHER SUPERIOR has heard

nothing. She stands in the centre of the stage
gazing at her bejewelled hands and arms.
SISTER INES enters, ghastly pale, and making
gestures of horror. She goes up to the MOTHER
SUPERIOR and shakes her, trying to pull her
over to the right).

MOTHER SUPERIOR. What's the matter with you,
child? Leave me alone: you're going to spoil
the jewels!

(SISTER INES points towards the right and tries
again to drag the MOTHER SUPERIOR in that
direction).

MOTHER SUPERIOR. What's happening? Isn't it
over yet?

(SISTER INES points desperately to the jewels
and the SENORA's cape, then puts her hands
round her neck and mimes the struggles of
somebody being strangled).

MOTHER SUPERIOR. And what do you expect me to
do about it? It isn't anybody's fault ... Things
happen because they have to happen: all the
books tell you that. Get that into your head and
you'll live a happier life. You mustn't think
about it, little Ines, you mustn't think about it.
Besides, it was either her ... or these. (She
points to the jewels which she has taken off one
by one) You can understand that, can't you?
As Sister Angelo would say (pronouncing the
name in the Italian fashion), you must never
hesitate about that sort of thing. (She starts
putting the jewels away) Oh, those drums!

They're like souls in torment! I can't wait to
get away from them. (Chants softly) Kyrie
eleison, kyrie eleison ...

(Seeing that she can't persuade her, SISTER INES
seizes the MOTHER SUPERIOR's hands and
tries to drag her away. Some of the jewels fall
to the ground).

MOTHER SUPERIOR. Let go, you little fool! Now look
what you've done! (She slaps SISTER INES's
face and bends down to pick up the jewels) You
don't think, do you? The work of several gen-
erations, and you throw it on the ground. Why,
you're so stupid that you don't even know the
meaning of respect!

(While the MOTHER SUPERIOR is picking
up the jewels, SISTER INES hunts around desperately until she finds a knife and then rushes
off towards the right. The drums start beating
frantically. From now on some of the dialogue
will be lost as the characters shout at one
another).

MOTHER SUPERIOR. (nervously putting the rest of
the jewels back in the small chest) Everybody's going mad ... The world's going to
pieces ... Nobody respects our rulers any
more and now we can see the consequences ...
A strong arm and a firm hand ... that's what
the law should be ... so that people can live
in peace ... Oh, if they'd only let me run the
country, I'd show them! ... Damn that noise!
It's getting on my nerves! I'd like to be on the
boat too and away from here!

SISTER ANGELA. (offstage) Let go, you little bitch!
I said let go!

MOTHER SUPERIOR. Now what's going on?

(There is the noise of packing-cases falling
down).

SISTER ANGELA. (offstage, in a choking voice) You'll
pay for this! (The rest is unintelligible).

MOTHER SUPERIOR. (running to the right) There's
never a moment's peace in this place ... What's
the matter now?

(She stops in the doorway. There is the sound
of blows and now and then the noise of a
packing-case being knocked over. The cries
which can be heard have nothing human about
them: they sound like the growls of wild beasts.
Outside the drums are still beating, and now
church bells can be heard in full peal).

MOTHER SUPERIOR. What's going on? What are
you doing? Oh, no! ... Not that! ... Look
out! ... Don't do that! You'll ... oh, no-o-o-o
(She turns away, shutting her eyes, and draws
back from the door, beating her head with her
fists) Idiot ... idiot ... idiot ...

SISTER ANGELA. (enters out of breath, with some
of her clothing torn and her coif thrown back)
She came at me from behind, like a puma ...
if I hadn't fought her off, she'd have killed me
... And all because of a smile and a present

from that bitch of a Senora ... Well, the smile
I shoved down her throat ... and I've kept the
present as a souvenir ... (She shows the cross).

MOTHER SUPERIOR. (drawing back) Things like
that mustn't happen! They'll bring us bad luck.
We mustn't fight among ourselves. We've
enough to do fighting the rest of the world! But
you've got to go and louse it all up ... Can't
you control your evil impulses like everybody
else? You stupid bitch! (She throws herself on
SISTER ANGELA to beat her up).

SISTER ANGELA. (dodges the blow, gives the MOTHER
SUPERIOR a punch, and then stands stock
still) Stop! (Cocks her head) You hear that?

MOTHER SUPERIOR. I can hear it all right. I've
heard it for some time ... But I don't want to
hear it!

SISTER ANGELA. Something must have happened!
When the bells and drums sound together!

MOTHER SUPERIOR. It's the evil eye ... bad luck
... Somebody's against us because things
were going too well for us.

SISTER ANGELA. Start getting our things together!
Get everything ready! I'm going to see what's
happening. If the road's clear we'll go where
the boat's waiting and leave before dawn ...

(SISTER ANGELA pulls her coif forward while
striding towards the left).

MOTHER SUPERIOR. Bad luck always strikes when
things are going well. (She goes out and comes
back almost immediately with a heavy sack
which she puts down in the centre of the stage.
The drums go on beating and the bells ringing
at full peal) You can never enjoy the fruits of
your labours in peace ... What matters is work
and brains ... planning and plotting in a world
full of idiots ... And when everything works
out and the jewels arrive ... Bang! ... What's
happened to those bells?

(The bells have in fact just stopped ringing.
The drums go on beating, but now on a happy
note.
The MOTHER SUPERIOR goes out again).

SISTER ANGELA. (shouting frantically offstage)
Hell! I've seen Hell! It's Hell out there!

(A panic-stricken SISTER ANGELA rushes in
from the left almost at the same time as the
MOTHER SUPERIOR comes in from the right,
dragging a heavy sack).

SISTER ANGELA. The whole town's burning ... The
church ... the town hall ... the barracks ...
People are running for their lives, with horrible
wounds ... No! ... No! ... I saw a man holding
his guts in his hands ... a woman carrying a
headless child ... Everything's burning ...
The whole town's going to be destroyed ...
There'll be nobody left ...

MOTHER SUPERIOR. (running over to the small
chest and pressing it to her body) It isn't true!

It can't be true!

SISTER ANGELA. But I've seen it! I've just seen it
with my own eyes ... We couldn't get to the
end of the street without getting our heads
chopped off ... We'd never make it to the beach!

MOTHER SUPERIOR. (huddling up in the centre of
the stage and hugging the chest in her arms)
It can't be true! It was just a story I made up
to frighten the Senora!

SISTER ANGELA. (laughing, spinning around and
skipping about) Yes, it was all planned down
to the smallest detail! A few weeks down here,
holed up like rats ... Then the Senora comes
along with her jewels ... The Senora with her
soft hands and her sharp nails ... The Senora
who doesn't want to die (somebody starts
hammering on the door) and fights and scratches
till the last breath is squeezed out of her ...
Everything's ready ... the boat's waiting for
us ... And off we go, sailing into the dawn.

MOTHER SUPERIOR. (with a little shriek) They're
here! They're hammering on the door! ... No,
it can't be true! ... No! ... (Pinches herself).

SISTER ANGELA. And we'll spend all our money
living it up! (Louder hammering on the door)
The heirs of a dead Senora! (She doubles up
with laughter) And now here they come ...
Hundreds of them ... Thousands of them ...
And it's all over ... all over!

MOTHER SUPERIOR. They aren't here! Nothing's
happened! Somebody's cast a spell on us to

make us think it's happened ... (Holding the
chest in one hand she makes the sign of the
Cross with the other against the evil eye)
Vade retro, Satane ... Vade retro!

SISTER ANGELA. Life was going to be one long
holiday for us ... A bright future full of idleness and peace!

(The sound of the drums grows louder, almost
drowning their voices. The knocking on the
door has stopped, but smoke starts pouring in
from the left).

MOTHER SUPERIOR. (on her knees, clasping the
chest in her arms) They're trying to make me
think they've set fire to the place, and I'm going
to be burnt alive! That's what I told the Senora
it was going to be like ... I said it would happen
just like that! But I don't want it to happen! I don
want it to happen! (She starts crying) Wake me u

SISTER ANGELA. (laughing crazily and coughing
from the smoke) One long holiday from morning
till night ... A holiday! ... A holiday!

(She starts singing a hymn in Hebrew at the top
of her voice).

MOTHER SUPERIOR. (screaming) Wake me up! For
God's sake wake me up!!!

(Smoke).

QUICK CURTAIN

PART TWO

(The stage looks as if a tornado had hit it.
Furniture is piled up against the door on the
left. The sacks the MOTHER SUPERIOR
dragged in during Part One have been ripped
open, and their contents are scattered over
the stage. The MOTHER SUPERIOR, her
robes torn and filthy, her head shaven, is
rummaging feverishly among the packing cases).

MOTHER SUPERIOR. (squatting among the packing-
cases and muttering to herself) All this trouble
because she got everything ready! If we'd gone
out to sea, it would have been just the same!
Nothing to eat and rubbish galore. Rags ...
and dolls ... the stupid bitch ... (Speaking to
SISTER INES, who has a bloodstained bandage
round her head and is crouching among a pile
of packing-cases and overturned furniture)
As for you, stop jittering and give me a hand
... Come on, it's not as bad as all that ...
(She shakes her and practically drags her
forward) You had a close shave, you know.
Now listen to what I'm going to tell you: don't
you go near her if you know what's good for
you! She's as crazy as a coot. And no wonder.
Those drums are enough to drive anybody mad.
Come on, you bloody parasite, start hunting!
She swore we'd have enough to eat for a
month at sea, and look at us now! Not a crumb
left.

54

(She suddenly stops rummaging about and
sits down with her legs apart, her elbows on
her knees and her head in her hands).

God Almighty, what's going to happen to us?

(SISTER INES has scarcely moved. She is
crawling around on all fours looking for food.
The silence is broken only by the occasional
sound of drums in the distance and an inter-
mittent chanting which sounds like a wail.
SISTER ANGELA comes in, head down, with
the sleeves of her habit torn off to show her
muscular arms, and her skirts in rags tied
up to look like a pair of trousers. SISTER
ANGELA is covered in dust and her arms
and hands are cut and grazed).

SISTER ANGELA. (looking at the MOTHER SUPERIO
from upstage) I suppose you're going to leave
me to do all the dirty work as usual?

MOTHER SUPERIOR. (not looking up) What do you
want me to do?

SISTER ANGELA. (coming closer) Go and do a bit
of digging for a change. I'm done in.

MOTHER SUPERIOR. I suppose life is just a garden
of roses for me?

SISTER ANGELA. All I know is, you do nothing but
sit on your ass. (She starts hunting around
where she kept her rum in Part One) And I
have to do the work for both of us.

MOTHER SUPERIOR. Believe me, I'm very
grateful.

SISTER ANGELA. (opens the bottle, puts it to her
mouth, tips it up, and then advances on the
MOTHER SUPERIOR in a fury) You've drunk
it all, damn you!

MOTHER SUPERIOR. (trying to avoid her) I used a
bit of it for poor Ines. You don't realize what
a mess you made of the girl ... I had to use
a little alcohol on the wound.

SISTER ANGELA. (stopping the MOTHER SUPERIOR)
Open your mouth! I want to smell! Come on now,
open up!

MOTHER SUPERIOR. (fighting to free herself) Let
me go! All right, so I took a swig of it. So
what? We're holed up here like rats in a trap,
with nothing to eat. So if there's something to
drink I've as much right to it as you have.

SISTER ANGELA. (leaning over the MOTHER SUPERIOR)
Nobody's got any rights here but me! I slog
my guts out and then you go and ...

MOTHER SUPERIOR. Shut up! Listen!

(The two of them freeze in the position they
were in when the MOTHER SUPERIOR spoke).

SISTER ANGELA. You think you heard them again?

MOTHER SUPERIOR. I'm positive.

SISTER ANGELA. (listening hard) I can't hear
　　　nothing.

MOTHER SUPERIOR. (freeing herself and going to
　　　add a few odds and ends to the barricade in
　　　front of the door) You didn't hear anything the
　　　other times either. But they knocked then
　　　like they did just now - as if they weren't
　　　sure of themselves.

　　　(Naturally there has been no noise. But seeing
　　　what the MOTHER SUPERIOR is doing, SISTER
　　　ANGELA also picks up a few planks and helps
　　　her to reinforce the barricade).

SISTER ANGELA. Why do they knock on the door?
　　　Why don't they break it down and get it over
　　　with?

MOTHER SUPERIOR. (going to the barricade) How
　　　should I know? Maybe they're testing our nerve
　　　... Maybe they're waiting for us to come out.
　　　(She picks up something near SISTER INES
　　　and shakes her) Come on, you! Give us a hand!
　　　We're all in the same boat.

　　　(SISTER INES starts picking up a few small,
　　　useless objects, with the expression and
　　　gestures of a sleepwalker, while taking care
　　　to avoid SISTER ANGELA).

SISTER ANGELA. (bringing over more material for
　　　the barricade, her activity increasing while
　　　the MOTHER SUPERIOR's slows down and
　　　SISTER INES's remains virtually non-existent)
　　　If they do get in, they've still got to catch us

... And I've a little surprise waiting for
them ... Take a look at this. (She stops
working and from her skirts pulls out a long
knife with a jagged blade) I fixed it myself.
Oh, they won't get me that easy. (SISTER
INES has jumped backwards in terror. The
MOTHER SUPERIOR also draws away, but
more discreetly. SISTER ANGELA gives a
sinister cackle) I've seen a man carve up a
whole platoon with a knife like that. (She
puts away the knife and goes on piling up
packing-cases. The MOTHER SUPERIOR
sits down wearily. SISTER INES curls up
again) But we won't need to do any fighting. By
the time they get in here we'll have finished
digging the tunnel. We've got out of worse
holes than this. Why can't we do it again? (She
stands still and listens hard) They're still
singing, but they aren't celebrating no more.

MOTHER SUPERIOR. What do you mean?

SISTER ANGELA. I mean something's happening out
there.

(Silence).

MOTHER SUPERIOR. I can't hear any difference.

SISTER ANGELA. (still listening hard) No. Something's happened to upset them. Maybe they're
mourning somebody who's died.

MOTHER SUPERIOR. (shouting all of a sudden) I
don't care whether they're mourning or celebrating ... if only they'd shut up! That singing

gets me right down in the guts. (Gets up and turns right round twice like a dog just before it lies down) And that smell!

SISTER ANGELA. (turning round, suddenly very calm and relaxed, and throwing herself down on a pile of sacks) She doesn't smell no more. She's buried good and deep.

MOTHER SUPERIOR. But you waited too long to bury her: you let her infect the whole place.

SISTER ANGELA. Don't you start bitching. You wouldn't even touch her. And I couldn't dig a tunnel and a grave at the same bloody time. When it comes to the crunch it's always me who has to do all the dirty work.

MOTHER SUPERIOR. (following her own train of thought) Tell me: do you really think we'll manage to get out of here?

SISTER ANGELA. We're on the right track all right. The earth's getting softer.

MOTHER SUPERIOR. And out there?

SISTER ANGELA. What do you mean, out there?

MOTHER SUPERIOR. I mean: when we come out of the tunnel, what'll we find?

SISTER ANGELA. I know what I'm doing: we'll come out on the beach.

MOTHER SUPERIOR. (drawing nearer to SISTER

ANGELA, as excited as a child listening to
a story) And what if they're waiting for us?

SISTER ANGELA. Then we'll fight our way through.
(She sees alarm on the MOTHER SUPERIOR's
face) But they won't be there. They never keep
watch when they're mourning their dead. The
beach will be empty.

MOTHER SUPERIOR. And the boat?

SISTER ANGELA. (after only a moment's hesitation)
The boat will be there all right.

MOTHER SUPERIOR. They won't have found it?

SISTER ANGELA. It was in a good hiding-place.

MOTHER SUPERIOR. So we'll be able to sail away
as planned?

SISTER ANGELA. All our plans will work out fine.
We've got the stuff, haven't we? (She looks
meaningfully at the MOTHER SUPERIOR).

MOTHER SUPERIOR. (taking a packet wrapped in
rags out of the large pocket in her skirt) Here
it is: with your share intact.

SISTER ANGELA. Go on looking after it for me, will
you? It gets in the way when I'm working.

MOTHER SUPERIOR. (putting the packet away and
getting edgy) Angela, we've got to keep digging
to get out of here! Shall I go and do a bit?

SISTER ANGELA. Scrape at it with the pickaxe first, and pick the earth up in your hands. And watch out or the roof will cave in on top of you.
(The MOTHER SUPERIOR has disappeared. SISTER ANGELA goes on talking to her, not realising that she has gone) You're so ham-fisted I've got to keep on explaining everything from A to Z. And even then you louse it all up. Because once you start ... (She breaks off and listens) That must be one of their leaders they're mourning. Things are going badly for them, that's for sure. It'd be a good time to get out of here, if only ...

(There is a frantic shriek. SISTER ANGELA jumps to her feet. SISTER INES comes running in, followed by the MOTHER SUPERIOR waving her arms, and hides in a corner).

MOTHER SUPERIOR. You witch! You devil! I caught her red-handed! She was clawing at the ground with her bare hands! (Shouting at SISTER ANGELA) She was trying to dig up that corpse, that stinking carcass! (Choking with fury, she runs towards SISTER INES, who tries to crawl away) What do you want her for, you idiot? (She picks up SISTER INES who covers her head with her arms to avoid the MOTHER SUPERIOR's blows) Are you that hungry?

SISTER ANGELA. Why don't we dig her up?

MOTHER SUPERIOR. (who was raising one hand to strike SISTER INES, gradually lets it fall and draws back, muttering) No ... No ...

SISTER ANGELA. (advancing to the MOTHER
SUPERIOR and getting more and more excited)
We dig her up ... We hand her over ... We
say: Here she is! The dead woman ... the
white woman ... We killed her for you ...
so you'd forgive us ... because we're like
you are.

MOTHER SUPERIOR. But her eyes had already fallen
out ...

SISTER ANGELA. Her colour isn't our colour ...

MOTHER SUPERIOR. And her flesh was rotting ...

SISTER ANGELA. We're like you really ... This
isn't our real skin ... Our enemies pulled
that off and left us looking like this ...

MOTHER SUPERIOR. ... the worms were eating her
up ...

SISTER ANGELA. But your gods are our gods ...

MOTHER SUPERIOR. ... and her bowels were stinking ...

SISTER ANGELA. ... and we'll offer up sacrifices
just like you ...

MOTHER SUPERIOR. ... she'll fall to pieces if we
touch her ...

SISTER ANGELA. Never mind what we look like ...
we're your friends, your sisters ... (The
MOTHER SUPERIOR goes on shaking her

head) Yes, why don't we dig her up? (The
MOTHER SUPERIOR points desperately at
the door, SISTER ANGELA changes abruptly)
What, again? (The MOTHER SUPERIOR nods
silently. SISTER ANGELA jumps on her like
a tiger, grabs her by the shoulders, and starts
shaking her) Why don't I ever hear them?
(She lowers her voice, looking at the door
like the MOTHER SUPERIOR) You're sure
they're out there? (The MOTHER SUPERIOR
nods again. SISTER ANGELA lowers her
voice still further) Keep quiet. Shut your eyes.
Maybe they'll go away like they did before,
without finding us.

(The two of them remain motionless, their
eyes closed).

MOTHER SUPERIOR. They've gone.

SISTER ANGELA. (opening her eyes in relief, and
suddenly full of energy) I'm going to do some
digging.

MOTHER SUPERIOR. (quickly, before SISTER ANGELA
has time to go out) But what if it wasn't them?
(SISTER ANGELA turns round) What if was
somebody else? It could be, you know ...
Maybe some of the Governor's men were
left ... Maybe ...

SISTER ANGELA. (curtly) I've been out there. I
told you what I saw. The only thing to do is
to keep on digging.

(SISTER ANGELA goes out. The odd thing is

63

that she does not go in the same direction as
before but in another direction, and starts
digging in a place where she is visible to the
audience).

MOTHER SUPERIOR. (after turning around several
times, squats on the floor, takes out the
packet of jewels, puts it on the floor and opens
it. She starts stroking the jewels and counting
them) She thinks I haven't realised that she's
digging several tunnels to put me off the
track. She thinks she's the only one who knows
the way to the beach. (She laughs quietly) But
I've got my own route, and when she drops
with fatigue I'm going to dig my own tunnel.
I'll scrape the earth away with the pickaxe
and remove it very carefully so the roof
doesn't fall in. And I'll come out on the beach
right where the boat is hidden. And I'm the
one who's got the jewels, because they bother
her, they burn her up ... (INES has come
closer, fascinated by the jewels) What are
you doing? What do you want? (She hurriedly
does up the packet again) I had nothing to do
with what happened. I wasn't there. That's
important, so don't forget it. I know you can't
talk, but you understand, and you know how
to make people understand you. So you'll
point to me and say: She had nothing to do with
all that ... It was the other one ... The one
who's always messing things up ... (She
grabs SISTER INES who was trying to get
away) Listen, little Ines, I'll take you with me
and give you the cross ... the cross she gave
you ... and where we're going you'll be like

you used to be again: happy and hard-working
and always ready to help. (She thrusts her face
up against SISTER INES's) But you'll have to
change the look in your eyes, the look on your
face ... Things disappear, Ines, but people
stay ... (Lowers her voice to a conspiratorial
tone) That's why you've got to keep your eyes
open, like me ... Because there are those
people outside ... and her with her knife ...
You've got to be careful, Ines, you've got to
be careful ...

(SISTER ANGELA comes back and watches
the other two for a moment).

SISTER ANGELA. That's a big help, I must say ...
(The MOTHER SUPERIOR hurriedly draws
away from SISTER INES) We've got to get
out tonight. (She comes forward, stops again,
and listens) Something's happening out there.
Something's gone wrong with their plans. The
drums are sounding the alarm.

MOTHER SUPERIOR. Maybe the others are coming?

SISTER ANGELA. (putting her hands to her throat)
God I'm thirsty!

MOTHER SUPERIOR. I'm sure somebody's trying
to help, somewhere.

SISTER ANGELA. (making signs to SISTER INES)
Get me something to drink ... something to
eat.

(SISTER INES starts rummaging around all

over the place like a mouse).

MOTHER SUPERIOR. If they've killed all our people here, then others are bound to come to avenge them ... From the islands ... from the mainland ... And then our time will come.

SISTER ANGELA. What do you mean?

MOTHER SUPERIOR. Why, we're the only survivors. When the others arrive and we come out, who can accuse us of anything? Nobody. Because there's nobody left. And then ...

SISTER ANGELA. (rummaging about at the bottom of a packing-case) But there's several jobs they can get us for.

MOTHER SUPERIOR. (leaning towards SISTER ANGELA) And who's going to tell on us? The trees? The wind? You've been outside. You've seen what happened. You told me yourself: they're all dead! And Angelo (pronouncing the name in the Italian fashion like the late SENORA) ... the dead don't talk. (SISTER ANGELA has found what she was looking for: a cigar stub. She puts it between her lips and starts looking for some matches) Besides, now I come to think of it, that idea of yours wasn't bad ... but only if we use it on the other side.

SISTER ANGELA. (still trying to find the matches, stops, and looks up) What do you mean? What are you talking about?

MOTHER SUPERIOR. (squats down too, so that both
        are facing the audience) We've got the Senora's
        corpse (gesturing in the direction of the
        SENORA's grave) We managed to get it back
        from those murdering savages. We kept the
        body with us to pay homage to it while we
        waited to be rescued. (Sees SISTER ANGELA's
        incredulous expression) You don't realize how
        important things like that are to those people.
        I've been with them, and I know. The Senora
        wasn't just the Senora, she was a family, a
        fortune, a name ...

SISTER ANGELA. But you said yourself she's
        nothing but a stinking carcass now.

MOTHER SUPERIOR. I was wrong! (Stands up) Only
        the poor stink when they die.

SISTER ANGELA. (standing up too) No. (She turns
        her back on the MOTHER SUPERIOR and
        goes looking for her matches somewhere
        else).

MOTHER SUPERIOR. (following her) Why not?

SISTER ANGELA. (coming back) Because all your
        ideas come a cropper in the end.

MOTHER SUPERIOR. (still following her) That isn't
        my fault. Oh, I know we've had a bit of bad
        luck now and then.

        (All the nuns are on the move, SISTER INES
        crawling about on all fours, SISTER ANGELA
        looking for her matches at the other end of

the stage, and the MOTHER SUPERIOR
following her around).

SISTER ANGELA. But this time, I'm the one who's
giving the orders.

MOTHER SUPERIOR. And I'm taking them, Angela.
Oh, I agree you're the one who always does
things the right way. But you can't deny I've
come up with some good ideas in the past
And after all, if what's happened hadn't
happened, we'd be out at sea now, with the
jewels.

SISTER ANGELA. (turning towards the MOTHER
SUPERIOR) So we dig her up. What then?

MOTHER SUPERIOR. (seizing the opportunity
offered by this change of attitude) We dress
her in all her finery. We do her up like a
queen. Then we bring her out when they arrive
and say: Here she is. We couldn't save her,
though we risked our lives trying to defend
her; but at least nobody violated her corpse.
(Drawing nearer to SISTER ANGELA) You
know what that means to them? It means that
we preserved order and tradition in the midst
of chaos. And because we did that, we can ask
them for anything we like.

SISTER ANGELA. Rum.

MOTHER SUPERIOR. Ham.

SISTER ANGELA. Cheese.

MOTHER SUPERIOR. And salad.

SISTER ANGELA. Good wines.

MOTHER SUPERIOR. Cakes from Holland.

SISTER ANGELA. A roast pig.

MOTHER SUPERIOR. Luscious fruit.

SISTER ANGELA. And more wine.

MOTHER SUPERIOR. Perhaps a drop of brandy.

SISTER ANGELA. Some tasty lamb ... a bit of game .

MOTHER SUPERIOR. And cigars ... skilfully rolled
... with a delicate aroma.

(The items in this list have been rattled off
one after another. Now the two nuns remain
motionless).

SISTER ANGELA. And we'll ask for a ship with a
thousand oars to take us across the sea fast,
very fast ...

MOTHER SUPERIOR. And when we get to the other
side, they'll give us a royal welcome.

SISTER ANGELA. Let's go! (She starts walking).

MOTHER SUPERIOR. (not moving) Where?

SISTER ANGELA. To dig her up.

MOTHER SUPERIOR. (drawing back) I can't.

SISTER ANGELA. (advancing on the MOTHER
SUPERIOR and grabbing her by the arm) It
was your idea. (She starts twisting the MOTHER
SUPERIOR's arm behind her back).

MOTHER SUPERIOR. (twisting her body to reduce
the pain) Talking's one thing ... Just sugges-
ting an idea ... But carrying it out's different
... Don't make me do it!

SISTER ANGELA. (twisting her arm a little further)
So I've got to be Jack-of-all-trades, have I?
Maid ... labourer ... gravedigger.

MOTHER SUPERIOR. (still writhing about, points
to SISTER INES) Take her with you! She's
already tried to dig her up! Well, now she
can do it! I'm no good for a job like that ...
I'm just a useless old thing ... You're the
one who knows how to plan everything ... do
everything ... with your brains ... your
strength ...

SISTER ANGELA. (pushing the MOTHER SUPERIOR
away from her) You make me sick! But don't
start bitching later on when I get the reward
and you get damn all. (She spins round, grabs
SISTER INES by the neck and practically
drags her across the stage ...) Come on,
you ... We've got work to do ... And no
monkey business this time ... And stop
wriggling, or I'll make sure you never
wriggle again ...

(SISTER ANGELA makes for the place where
the SENORA is buried. Drags SISTER INES
with her.
The MOTHER SUPERIOR starts rummaging
about among the sacks).

MOTHER SUPERIOR. Now, how should we dress to
welcome the new arrivals? In our best clothes,
or the rags we're wearing now? (She starts
unfolding nuns' coifs, skirts and habits) We
could appear in all the dignity of our calling
... But perhaps they ought to see us as we
are now, bearing the visible marks of our
sufferings ... (She takes out a few pieces of
clothing and strokes them) We'll keep our
best clothes for the moment of triumph when
our devotion has been recognised and we are
received at the Governor's palace. We'll
walk across thick carpets towards a brightly
lit drawing-room, and as we approach, the
guests will fall silent as a mark of respect ...
The Governor will bow to us and make a speech
telling how we defended the life and honour of
a noble lady. Then he'll decorate us with the
Order of Merit, and afterwards there won't
be any festivities, out of respect for the
martyr's memory, but a delicious collation
served with quiet good taste in the Residency
gardens ... (As well as the nuns' habits the
MOTHER SUPERIOR takes out a few unexpec-
ted articles - men's trousers? masks? -
mixed up so that the audience may not see
what they are) We'll tell those good people
all about the horrors we've lived through ...
the revolution ... the blood ... the sleep-
less nights ... the dead with their heads

chopped off ... their bodies mutilated by those
monsters ...

SISTER ANGELA. (shouting from offstage) Come
back here, you idiot! You can't leave me with
it half-way out! Send her back here!

(SISTER INES, who has been helping SISTER
ANGELA to dig up the SENORA, comes in,
runs up to the MOTHER SUPERIOR, and
begins miming what she saw in Part One: the
murder of the SENORA).

MOTHER SUPERIOR. What's the matter? What's
got into you? What are you trying to say?
(She does not understand or refuses to understand what SISTER INES is trying to explain
to her, until she is forced to give in to the
nun's persistence) Don't get so worked up, you
silly fool! It isn't that! Don't you understand?
(She takes her by the shoulders and tries to
calm her down) That's all over ... it's ancient
history ... Now it's different ... it's something else ... Go back to Angela ... Go and
give her a hand ... You see, we're going to
dress up your Senora ... We're going to do
her up like a Madonna ... make her look
beautiful so we can show her to her friends and
relations ... We'll say: Here she is ...
doesn't she look as if she's asleep? ... And
they'll say: She looks just like she did the last
time we saw her ... a little paler ... a little
quieter ... but just the same ... We can see
she's been properly cared for, well looked
after ... Go on, now ... Don't make Sister
Angela angry! ... (Lowering her voice) You

know how furious she gets when she's crossed
... I don't want any more trouble ... So off
you go like a good girl ...

(While the MOTHER SUPERIOR has been
talking to SISTER INES downstage, trying to
convince her by word and gesture, ANGELA
has been dragging the corpse in and propping
it up in a niche in the wall).

SISTER ANGELA. She weighs more now than when
she was alive ... And she stinks like a cess-
pool ... Oh, you think up some good ideas,
you do ... Show anybody this hunk of meat and
he'll run a mile ... We'll have to do a real
good job on her if anybody's going to think we
treated her right ... What do we tell em?
She died in the odour of sanctity, but don't
get too close, mate, because you've never
known a stink like the smell of a dead saint ...
All right! One of you two come and give me a
hand!

MOTHER SUPERIOR. (picking out from the clothes
she has unpacked the cape the SENORA wore
in Part One) Look ... take her that, so she
looks beautiful ... Go on ... Get a move on
... (She pushes SISTER INES away and comes
back to the clothes and other articles she has
scattered about on the floor) We ought to tidy
this up ... get ready to go at a moment's notice
... What a mess we've made! What a muddle!

SISTER ANGELA. (to SISTER INES, at the same
time as the MOTHER SUPERIOR) Give me
that! (She takes the cape) Now hold her while

I put it on ... (To SISTER INES, who is
holding the corpse steady) Hold her steady,
you ninny, or she'll fall over ... The dress is
all torn and filthy dirty, but the cape'll hide
all that ... We'll have to comb her hair too
... And do something to her face, I reckon ...

MOTHER SUPERIOR. (folding and putting away all
the clothes) When our people have arrived and
everything's over and we can go out again,
we'll have plenty of time to put on our best
clothes ... We've got to make a show of
poverty now and then so that people feel sorry
for us and help us, but we mustn't overdo it ...
people hate to see long faces and weepy eyes
... After the tears we must smile again,
laugh again ... But what's this? (Finding a
small box, she opens it and takes out a little
bottle. She uncorks it, sniffs it, tastes the
contents: some sort of alcoholic drink. She
darts a glance at SISTER ANGELA and, seeing
that she is busy with the corpse, takes a
long swig at the bottle. She then puts it away
inside her skirts) Laughter opens every heart
and every door. Oh, I hope they come and
save us soon so that we can all laugh again!

SISTER ANGELA. (at the same time as the MOTHER
SUPERIOR's monologue) The worms have
already eaten her eyes away and half her
nose ... There's nothing like death for showing
the living they're made of shit ... Hold her
steady, you idiot!

MOTHER SUPERIOR. (still putting the clothes away)
After I've had a really good meal, I swear

I'm going to lie down on a nice soft bed and laugh ... just laugh ...

SISTER ANGELA. Give me a veil, a scarf, one of those jewels ... We've got to do her up nice and pretty ...

MOTHER SUPERIOR. (surprised by SISTER ANGELA's arrival, starts rummaging feverishly in the sacks) Veils ... scarves ... something pretty ... Let's see ... What about this mantilla? ... It was among her things ... I'd say it was worth quite a bit.

SISTER ANGELA. It'll do. (She looks at some of the other articles) What about that?

MOTHER SUPERIOR. This peineta? You think it's suitable?

SISTER ANGELA. She's got to have something to keep her hair up.

MOTHER SUPERIOR. (prepared to argue, but seeing SISTER ANGELA's outstretched hand) All right ... But I'd prefer to keep it ... We could get a good price for it: it's hand made. The Senora certainly didn't stint herself ...

SISTER ANGELA. And one of those jewels ...

MOTHER SUPERIOR. (pretending not to have heard, walks to another part of the stage) Have you seen what a mess we've made?

SISTER ANGELA. (shouting) Give me a bracelet ...
a necklace ... a pair of earrings ...

MOTHER SUPERIOR. (shouting too) What for? What
good will it do her?

SISTER ANGELA. It's so they can't say we robbed
her. Who's going to believe we looked after
her just for love if she's wearing none of her
jewels?

MOTHER SUPERIOR. Jewels can drop off and get
lost ...

SISTER ANGELA. (advancing on the MOTHER SUPERIOR)
Give them to me!

MOTHER SUPERIOR. (drawing back) All right, all
right ... I'll look for something ...

SISTER ANGELA. (catching her) Hand them over!
I'll take what I need ...

(She snatches the packet from the MOTHER
SUPERIOR and moves away).

MOTHER SUPERIOR. You brute! You don't know how
to behave like a decent human being!

SISTER ANGELA. (opening the packet and laughing)
You're a fool to be stingy like that. Can't
you get it into your thick head you've got to
give a bit to get a lot?

MOTHER SUPERIOR. (choking with fury) You just
throw things away. You forget all the sweat

and blood they've cost us.

SISTER ANGELA. (picking the jewels up in both
hands and letting them fall) These little
beauties haven't cost you a drop of sweat ...
or blood either ... Now let's see ... What
would look best on the Senora? ... This
bracelet for a start ...

MOTHER SUPERIOR. You're throwing away our
riches, Angela ...

SISTER ANGELA. These rings ...

MOTHER SUPERIOR. Don't throw them away too ...

SISTER ANGELA. Maybe this necklace ...

MOTHER SUPERIOR. (stretching out her hands as
if trying to protect the jewels) You might at
least pick some of the cheaper stuff ...

SISTER ANGELA. (slapping her hard on both hands,
so that she pulls them back with a grimace of
pain) I'm giving the orders here! When I've
finished the Senora's going to look like a
queen! And this tiara'll give the finishing
touch ... Has that idiot let her fall again?
(Seeing SISTER INES struggling to keep the
corpse upright) I'm coming, you ninny, hang
on! (Goes upstage towards the corpse).

MOTHER SUPERIOR. (advances down stage holding
the packet of jewels in her hands as if it were
a baby) If she had her way, we'd give the whole

lot back. (She starts counting the jewels, stroking them gently) I ought to have lied to her, and told her I'd lost them all ... But these I'm going to hide ... She can do what she likes with her share, I'm keeping mine ... I'll swallow them if need be ... Sooner or later we'll get out of here ... I've prayed hard, and prayers are always answered when they come from the heart ... Lord, oh, Lord bring this nightmare to an end ... St. Anthony, rescue us from this prison ... Immaculate Heart of Mary, help us in our sorrows ... St. Blaise, who could do anything you chose, cure us of our fears ... St. Assumption, listen to your servant ... St. Isidore, protect me from danger, deliver me from evil ... save me from evil ... part me from evil ... banish the evil eye ... evil spirits ... evil thoughts ... save your servant ... save your ewe-lamb ... save your faithful follower ... save her body from attack ... save her flesh from greedy fingers ... Evil is everywhere, waiting and watching ... soaking into your pores ... creeping into your dreams ... sticking to your bowels ... Save your servant from evil ... St. Eustache ... St. Teresa ... St. Bernard ... save me ... deliver me from evil ... save me ... (At the beginning of this litany she hid the jewels in her skirts, and while reciting it she has been facing the audience and performing a whole series of actions, genuflecting, beating her breast, etc.)

SISTER ANGELA. (at the same time, her voice providing a background to the MOTHER SUPERIOR's litany) She's beginning to look a

bit better already ... Let's put on her jewels
to brighten things up a bit ... This peineta's
a good idea, to keep the hair out of her eyes ...
She needs a bit of powder and paint as well,
or at least a spot of rouge ... We've got to
cover up that rotting flesh somehow ... They'll
have to come down here to see her anyway,
because if we take her outside she'll come apart
in our hands ... Sunshine's no good for you if
you aren't fit and healthy ... (To SISTER INES)
Hold her up while I try and push her back a
bit ... Now how about that? There's your
Senora again, as good as new ... Just like
she was when she came here, with her airs
and graces ... (Changing her voice to imitate
the SENORA) Heavens above! What a dreadful
place! How on earth do you manage to live
down here, Reverend Mother? (With an angry
shove which would have pushed the corpse
over if SISTER INES had not lovingly held it
up) How did we manage to live down here?
How could we stand it? I'd have told her all
right! When you've been hounded all your life
any place with a roof on it is fine! When you're
used to fighting like a rat in a trap, nobody's
got the right to shovel pity over you! I didn't
talk to her, but I shut her mouth for good and
all. (Faces the corpse and addresses it) Now
look at you, in all your laces and silks! Look
at you now, you old bag, you lump of rotten
meat! (She steps back like a painter inspecting
her work) Though I say it myself, she looks
pretty good. I've done a good job there ...
(To SISTER INES) Now you look after her!
(Going over to the MOTHER SUPERIOR) Come
on, make yourself useful ... Cut me a bit of

this rope. (She hands the MOTHER SUPERIOR
her knife. There is something between them
which forces SISTER ANGELA to bow as she
hands the knife to the MOTHER SUPERIOR,
who is still in the midst of her prayers and
obeys without thinking).

MOTHER SUPERIOR. Save us from drowning in the
bottomless pit of evil ... Amen ... Amen ...
(After cutting the rope and giving it to SISTER
ANGELA, she puts the knife down in full view
of the audience. SISTER ANGELA goes back
upstage) When all this is over, I'll change, I
swear I will. And I'll do penance for my sins.
I'll give things to the poor. That's the best
way of keeping the saints on your side. When
they're happy they leave you in peace, and
that's what I need most of all: peace and quiet.
A quiet life somewhere in the country where
nothing ever moves. That's what I want. If
the world didn't move, as they say it does,
things would be so much better. It's all this
hustle and bustle that messes things up. If
only human beings were stones and statues,
how peaceful it would be!

SISTER ANGELA. (at the same time as the MOTHER
SUPERIOR, to SISTER INES) Come on, you
fool, lend me a hand. We've got to tie her
up ... There now, sitting there with all her
sparklers she looks quite different. Now for
her mantilla ... that'll hide the bit of her face
that's rotting away ... And we're already
getting used to the smell ... We're made that
way: put a man in hell and after a couple of

weeks he'll be used to it ... The main thing
is staying alive ... There now ... the peineta
a bit to one side ... She reminds me of a
picture I saw in the church back home ...
when I was a kid ... A lovely lady with a
mantilla, a peineta and a string of jewels ...
God, I loved that picture ... And she was dead
too. (Turning towards the MOTHER SUPERIOR)
Come and have a look ... Have I done a good job
on her, or haven't I?

MOTHER SUPERIOR. (looking over her shoulder,
not very enthusiastically) Yes, I can see from
here ... Jolly good ... Bravo ...

SISTER ANGELA. I said come and have a look! ...
She may be missing something.

MOTHER SUPERIOR. (approaching reluctantly) You
don't need me, Angela. Anybody can see it's
a masterpiece. I always said you had an
artistic soul.

(While the MOTHER SUPERIOR is approaching
the corpse, SISTER INES creeps over to the
place where the knife is lying, but without
intending to touch it as yet).

SISTER ANGELA. Now nobody can say we haven't
looked after her. Get an eyeful of that.

(SISTER INES spins round frantically as if
she were choking).

MOTHER SUPERIOR. Yes, I must admit she doesn't
look so bad done up like that ... I told you it

was a good idea ... When the last shots have
been fired and our people are victorious,
we'll go out into the street ... (SISTER INES
suddenly spots the knife. SISTER ANGELA
lights a cigar stub) And you know what? ...
I think we ought to take her with us ...
(SISTER INES picks up the knife) Oh, I know
she's heavy and stinks to high heaven, but if
all three of us carry her - you and me and
little Ines - (SISTER INES advances on the
other two, who are completely unsuspecting,
with the knife raised in the air) We'd create
quite an effect. Three sweet little nuns carrying
the mortal remains of a noble lady ... Why,
you silly thing, you don't wear a peineta on
that side ...

(The MOTHER SUPERIOR goes towards the
corpse to move the peineta. SISTER INES
springs forward to place herself between her
and the corpse, and lunges at her with the
knife, which the MOTHER SUPERIOR only
just avoids).

MOTHER SUPERIOR. What the ... ?

SISTER ANGELA. Get back!

(This time the knife was aimed at SISTER
ANGELA).

MOTHER SUPERIOR. Ines ... Ines, my child! ...
What's got into you?

(SISTER INES lunges at her again. The MOTHER

SUPERIOR jumps back).

SISTER ANGELA. (getting ready to fight, and crouching like a tiger about to spring) The little
bitch! I ought to have done her in back there!
But she'll pay for it now!

(SISTER ANGELA tries to trick SISTER INES
with a feint, but SISTER INES lunges at her
and she has to throw herself to one side to
avoid the knife).

MOTHER SUPERIOR. (hiding behind a piece of
furniture) No, Ines, no! Calm down, dear!
Your mother's here who loves you! ... Drop
that nasty knife and come here to me ...

(SISTER INES seems to be listening to what
the MOTHER SUPERIOR is saying, but keeps
a wary eye on SISTER ANGELA. Consequently
when SISTER ANGELA tries a second time to
take her by surprise she fails again).

SISTER ANGELA. (to the MOTHER SUPERIOR in
tones of baffled rage) Don't stand there doing
nothing! Give me a hand! It'll take two of us
to catch her ... Try and get her from behind
...

(SISTER INES stands in front of the corpse,
protecting it, and lunging left and right with
the knife).

MOTHER SUPERIOR. We've got to win her over by
persuasion. She'll always do as I say. You
mustn't hurt her, Angela ...

SISTER ANGELA. All right, go ahead and persuade
        her ... Go on, and let's see what happens ...

MOTHER SUPERIOR. (coming out of her hiding
        place and approaching SISTER INES slowly,
        talking in her sweetest tone of voice) Come on
        now, Ines dear, that's quite enough of that ...
        Now you know what a mess we're in, don't
        you? ... Just think what's happening out
        there ... I tell you it's horrible: the Devil
        prowling about with his tail in the air ...
        blood flowing in all the houses. There isn't a
        single Christian left alive ... We're all alone
        ... Well, we've got to be nice to one another,
        haven't we ... we've got to love one another
        ... If we start quarrelling, what's going to
        happen? We'll be at the mercy of all those
        savages ... Drop that knife, dear. You've
        seen how pretty Angela's made the Senora ...
        When she hurt her earlier on, she didn't mean
        to, and now she's looking after her so that
        nobody ...

        (The MOTHER SUPERIOR has been advancing
        towards SISTER INES with one hand out-
        stretched to take the knife, and SISTER INES
        seemed ready to hand it over. When the
        MOTHER SUPERIOR has almost reached her,
        SISTER ANGELA, losing patience and think-
        ing she can take SISTER INES by surprise,
        slips between the sacks to attack her from
        behind. The attempt fails, and SISTER
        ANGELA and SISTER INES find themselves
        engaged in a desperate struggle).

MOTHER SUPERIOR. (shouting) You idiot! Couldn't
you wait till I'd got her knife? Now look what
you've done! That's enough! Ines! Angela!
Stop fighting! Look out! Oh, dear, they're
going to kill each other! ... Ines, listen to
me! Angela, that's enough! ... Do as I say,
damn you!

SISTER ANGELA. (while fighting) You little bitch ...
I'll teach you ... You just wait ... Take that!
... I'll get you for this ... There! ...

MOTHER SUPERIOR. (picking up a stick and hitting
out wildly at the other two) That's enough, I
said ... Get back to your places ... You're
going to break everything ... (Hitting harder)
You'll get hurt if you go on like this ... Stop
it! ... That's enough ... Now stop it, I said
... Angela! ... Ines ... Look out! ... The
Senora! ...

(Knocked sideways in the fight, the corpse
topples over. SISTER INES jumps to her
feet and stabs SISTER ANGELA. Seeing the
SENORA on the ground and SISTER ANGELA
bleeding, SISTER INES takes fright and falls
back, still holding the knife).

SISTER ANGELA. (shouting to the MOTHER SUPERIOR)
Grab her knife, quick! Now's your chance
while she's frightened ... She's nicked me,
and she's quite capable of killing us both ...
Nab her quick ...

MOTHER SUPERIOR. (advancing on SISTER INES
and now very angry) Come here, you wicked

girl! You've spoilt everything now ... Angela
won't forgive you this time ... and I'm losing
patience too ... (She takes a big cushion and
advances on SISTER INES behind this shield)
Be good to animals they say ... But this is
how you thank me for treating you kindly ...,
Well, this time I'm the one who's going to
punish you ... You're going to give me that
knife and then I'm going to give you a beating
that'll flay the skin off your backside ...
(SISTER INES falls back against a pile of furniture. The MOTHER SUPERIOR advances
slowly) Hand it over!

(The MOTHER SUPERIOR hurls herself on
SISTER INES who tries to stab her, but fails
on account of the cushion).

SISTER ANGELA.   (dressing her wound but following
the progress of the fight with passionate
interest) Hey! Watch out! ... Don't go straight
at her ... Get her from the side! ... Not
that way, you fool, she'll cut you to ribbons!
... That's right: Now you've got her trapped!
... You've just got to jump her! ... Don't let
her get away! ... That's the stuff ... Now
bash her, kick her! ... Look out, you're
going to lose your balance ... Take a breather!
Watch her left hand, it's dangerous! ... Push
her in the corner! Try and get her face! ...
One in the guts! ... Don't let her get her
breath back! ... That's right! You've got her
now! Don't let her go! ... Twist her arm if
she won't drop her knife ... Lean on her! ...
Lean on her hard!

86

(At this point SISTER ANGELA, who until
now has been commenting on the fight as if
it were a wrestling match, falls silent and
watches in tense fascination. The MOTHER
SUPERIOR has got SISTER INES on the ground
and is kneeling on her, holding her arms outstretched. The cushion is between them.
SISTER INES, who is still holding the knife,
gradually lets it slip from her fingers).

MOTHER SUPERIOR. (influenced by SISTER ANGELA'
running commentary) You filthy bitch! You
little whore! You've made me sweat more
today than I've done since I was twenty ...
And what for? ... You'll always be a loser
... The weak shouldn't ever fight the strong
or the intelligent ... Your function in life
was to keep quiet and stay in a corner until
you were called ... Instead of that, you dared
to raise your hand against me, and if I hadn't
stopped you, you'd have stuck a knife in my
guts ... You bitch! ... You louse! ... (SISTER
INES lies perfectly still, her eyes fixed on
the MOTHER SUPERIOR) Now what's got
into you? What are you looking at me like
that for? You think I ought to forgive you too?
Shut those eyes ... Don't look at me like
that! ... It gives me the shivers feeling sorry
for you! ... I told you to shut those eyes!
That's enough! ... (She puts the cushion over
SISTER INES face and presses down on it
with all her strength. SISTER INES arms flail
about for a time and then drop to the ground)
(This isn't my fault ... Maybe it isn't your
fault either ... The fact is, it isn't anybody's
fault, what's happened ... Something guides

obey ... All we do is follow ... We can't
prevent things from happening ...

(She gradually relaxes the pressure of her
arms. SISTER INES is already dead.
The MOTHER SUPERIOR slowly joins SISTER
ANGELA, near the footlights. SISTER ANGELA ,
who has not moved during the fight, sits down,
very relaxed).

MOTHER SUPERIOR.   (quietly) Maybe it's better
like this. Now nothing can hurt her any more
... (She sits down too. The drums and singing
have stopped since SISTER INES died. For the
first time since the beginning of Part Two
there is complete silence. SISTER ANGELA
lights another cigar stub. The MOTHER SUP-
ERIOR takes out the bottle she had found and
hidden, takes a swig and passes it to SISTER
ANGELA) Have a drink. This excitement's
very tiring.

SISTER ANGELA.   (with a vague gesture towards the
corpse) That one broke up when she fell.
Anyway, I don't think it was a good idea digging her up. People always want to know what's
been going on. And they always end up finding
out. We'll have to bury her again.

MOTHER SUPERIOR.   Yes. And get our jewels back.
The more we've got, the better ... (Taking
back the bottle SISTER ANGELA holds out to
her) Where we're going everything costs the
earth ... And we'll need a lot of things, an
awful lot of things ...

SISTER ANGELA. (taking out another cigar stub, lighting it from her own and handing it to the MOTHER SUPERIOR, who offers her the bottle again) Have a cigar. I knew a sailor once who used to say: You've got to smoke a lot to put a curtain of smoke around the world. That's your only hope of being happy. (She laughs).

MOTHER SUPERIOR. (beginning to smoke) It's ourselves we ought to put a curtain around, to protect us. And not smoke, either, but gates, railings, walls ... After all, you never can tell ...

SISTER ANGELA. (pursuing the same train of thought) ... He always smelt of gunpowder, baccy and rum ... A real man he was ... A hell of a fellow on land or sea.

MOTHER SUPERIOR. (following her train of thought) ... When I've sold my share, I think I'll buy myself a castle and put spikes on all the walls to keep everybody out ... I've seen enough people to last me a lifetime ... Pass the bottle ...

SISTER ANGELA. (still thoughtful) Listen!

MOTHER SUPERIOR. (putting the bottle to her lips but finding it empty) Finished! (She tosses the bottle aside).

SISTER ANGELA. (slowly getting to her feet, but still listening) You can't hear a thing.

MOTHER SUPERIOR. (standing up too) They must
       have gone away and left us ...

SISTER ANGELA. (without looking at her, un-
       consciously tries to touch the MOTHER
       SUPERIOR) Like the calm before the storm,
       when there isn't a leaf moving ...

MOTHER SUPERIOR. (without noticing, instinctively
       takes SISTER ANGELA's hand) They've gone.
       I can't say I'm surprised. They've no idea how
       to run things.

SISTER ANGELA. The quieter it is, the worse the
       storm when it comes ...

MOTHER SUPERIOR. They say that in the old days
       the natives of these islands used to paddle
       from one island to another in canoes ...

SISTER ANGELA. You hear that?

(There have been a few muffled blows).

MOTHER SUPERIOR. No, nothing.

SISTER ANGELA. Listen.

MOTHER SUPERIOR. (letting go of SISTER ANGELA's
       hand and drawing back slightly) I've a con-
       fession to make: that hammering on the door,
       I ... I made it up ... so that you'd leave me
       alone ... I could never tell with you ... You're
       so unpredictable ...

90

SISTER ANGELA. (going over to SISTER INES's
corpse to get the knife she had dropped. The
hammering on the door gradually grows louder)
They've come for us! ... This time they know
we're here ... (She picks up the knife and
makes sure the blade is sharp).

MOTHER SUPERIOR. (tying her skirts like SISTER
ANGELA's so that they look like trousers)
We think we can hear them now, but we can't
... They've gone away ... There's nobody on
the island ... We're all alone ...

SISTER ANGELA. (slipping the knife into her belt)
And they'll make us pay for what we've done,
and what we haven't done too! Well, I'm not
going to be a martyr for nobody! ... (Shouts
in sudden hysteria) I want to live!

(SISTER ANGELA stands for a moment, tense
and erect. There is a tremendous thump on
the door. The barricade begins to collapse.
SISTER ANGELA runs to the spot where she
was digging a tunnel at the beginning of Part
Two).

MOTHER SUPERIOR. (going up to the SENORA's
corpse, tearing off all the jewels, and hiding
them) Forgive me again! But there are exten-
uating circumstances ... Where I'm going ...
with all these jewels ... I'll pay a priest to
say Masses for your soul ... and I'll keep a
cameo in memory of you. (There is more
hammering on the door, the barricade shifts
a little more, and a strange noise is heard

like the beginning of an earthquake. SISTER
ANGELA goes on digging. The MOTHER
SUPERIOR runs towards the centre of the
stage and looks upwards left and right) Lord,
don't let anything happen to me! Don't hold a
grudge against me! I've already promised I'd
change! ... I believe in you! ... Don't refuse
me your forgiveness! (More of the barricade
collapses. The strange noise grows louder)
Angela! You're making a mistake! That isn't
the right way! Follow me! ... (She goes towards the place where she had begun digging
her tunnel) This is the way out! ... The light's
over there ... Just a little further! ...

(The MOTHER SUPERIOR starts digging frantically. SISTER ANGELA is already digging at
a frenzied rate. More of the barricade collapses. The strange sound grows louder and
louder until it is almost unbearable).

CURTAIN

C AND B PLAYSCRIPTS

		Cloth	Paper
* PS 1	TOM PAINE by Paul Foster	21s	6s6d
* PS 2	BALLS and other plays (The Recluse, Hurrah for the Bridge The Hessian Corporal) by Paul Foster	25s	7s6d
PS 3	THREE PLAYS (Lunchtime Concert, Coda The Inhabitants) by Olwen Wymark	21s	6s6d
* PS 4	CLEARWAY by Vivienne C. Welburn	21s	6s6d
* PS 5	JOHNNY SO LONG and THE DRAG by Vivienne C. Welburn	25s	8s6d
* PS 6	SAINT HONEY and OH DAVID, ARE YOU THERE? by Paul Ritchie	25s	10s6d
PS 7	WHY BOURNEMOUTH? and other plays (The Missing Links, An Apple a Day by John Antrobus	25s	10s0d
* PS 8	THE CARD INDEX and other plays (The Interrupted Act, Gone Out) by Tadeusz Rozewicz trans. Adam Czerniawski	25s	10s6d

		Cloth	Paper
PS 27	ANNA LUSE and other plays (Jens, Purity) by David Mowat	30s	15s0d
* PS 28	O and other plays by Sandro Key-Aarberg	25s	9s0d
* PS 29	WELCOME TO DALLAS, MR KENNEDY Kaj Himmelstrup	25s	9s0d
PS 30	THE LUNATIC, THE SECRET SPORTSMAN AND THE WOMEN NEXT DOOR and VIBRATIONS by Stanley Eveling	25s	9s0d
* PS 31	STRINDBERG Colin Wilson	21s	9s0d
* PS 32	THE FOUR LITTLE GIRLS by Pablo Picasso trans. Roland Penrose	25s	9s0d
PS 33	MACRUNE'S GUEVARA by John Spurling	25s	9s0d
* PS 34	THE MARRIAGE by Witold Gombrowicz trans. Louis Iribarne	25s	9s0d
* PS 35	BLACK OPERA and THE GIRL WHO BARKS LIKE A DOG by Gabriel Cousin trans. Irving Lycett	30s	15s0d

		Cloth	Paper
* PS 36	SAWNEY BEAN by Robert Nye and Bill Watson	25s	9s0d
PS 37	COME AND BE KILLED and DEAR JANET ROSENBERG, DEAR MRS KOONING by Stanley Eveling	25s	9s0d
PS 38	VIETNAM DISCOURSE by Peter Weiss trans. Geoffrey Skelton	25s	9s0d
* PS 39	HEIMSKRINGLA. or THE STONED ANGELS by Paul Foster	25s	9s0d
* PS 40	JAN PALACH by Alan Burns	25s	9s0d
* PS 41	HOUSE OF BONES by Roland Dubillard	25s	9s0d
* PS 42	THE TREADWHEEL and COIL WITHOUT DREAMS by Vivienne C. Welburn	25s	9s0d
PS 44	THE SLEEPERS DEN and OVER GARDENS OUT by Peter Gill	25s	9s0d

* All plays marked thus are represented for dramatic
  presentation by:
  C and B (Theatre) Ltd, 18 Brewer Street, London W1